JAN MARK
Eyes wide open

...strated by Scoular Anderson

A & C Black • London

First published 2003 by
A & C Black Publishers Ltd
37 Soho Square, London, W1D 3QZ

Contents

For Kade and Corey

Teeth

Eric still lives in the town where we grew up. He says he wants to stay close to his roots. That's a good one. You can say that again. Roots.

Some people are rich because they are famous. Some people are famous just for being rich. Eric Donnelly is one of the second sort, but I knew him before he was either, when we were at Victoria Road Primary together. I don't really know Eric any more, but I can read about him in the papers any time, same as you can. He was in one of the colour supplements last Sunday, with a photograph of his house all over a double-page spread. You need a double-page spread to take in Eric these days. He was being interviewed about the things he really considers important in life, which include, in the following order, world peace, conservation, foreign travel (to promote world peace, of course, not for *fun*), his samoyeds (a kind of very fluffy wolf) and his wife. He didn't mention money but anyone who has ever known Eric – for three years like I did or even for five minutes – knows that on Eric's list it comes at the top, way in front of world peace.

In the photo he was standing with the wife and three of the samoyeds in front of the house, trying to look ordinary. To *prove* how ordinary he is he was explaining how he used to be very poor and clawed his way up using only his own initiative. Well, that's true as far as it goes: his own initiative and his own claws – and other people's teeth. He didn't mention the teeth.

'Well,' says Eric modestly, in the Sunday supplement, 'it's a standing joke, how I got started. Cast-iron baths.' That too is true as far as it goes. When Eric was fifteen he got a job with one of those firms that specialize in house clearances. One day they cleared a warehouse which happened to contain two hundred and fifty Victorian cast-iron baths with claw feet. It occurred to Eric that there were a lot of people daft enough to actually want a Victorian bath with claw feet; people, that is, who hadn't had to grow up with them, so he bought the lot at a knock-down price, did them up and flogged them. That bit's well known, but in the Sunday supplement he decided to come clean. He came clean about how he'd saved enough money to buy the baths in the first place by collecting scrap metal, cast-offs, old furniture and returnable bottles. 'A kind of rag-and-bone man,' said Eric, with the confidence of a tycoon who can afford to admit that he used to be a rag-and-bone man because he isn't one any more. He still didn't mention the teeth.

I first met Eric Donnelly in the Odeon one Saturday morning during the kids' show. I'd seen him around at school before – he was in the year above mine – but here he was sitting next to me. I was trying to work out one of my front teeth which had been loose for ages and was now hanging by a thread. I could open and shut it, like a door, but it kept getting stuck and I'd panic in case it wouldn't go right side round again. In the middle of the millionth episode of *Thunder Riders* it finally came unstuck and shot out. I just managed to field it and after having a quick look I shoved it in my pocket. Eric leaned over and said in my earhole, 'What are you going to do with that, then?'

'Put it under me pillow,' I said. 'Me mum'll give me sixpence for it.'

'Oh, the tooth fairy,' said Eric. I hadn't quite liked to mention the tooth fairy. I was only eight but I knew already what happened to lads who went round talking about fairies.

'Give it to us, then,' Eric said. 'I'll pay you sixpence.'

'Do you collect them?' I asked him.

'Sort of,' said Eric. 'Go on – sixpence. What about it?'

'But me mum knows it's loose,' I said.

'Sevenpence, then.'

'She'll want to know where it went.'

'Tell her you swallowed it,' Eric said. 'She won't care.'

He was right, and I didn't care either, although I cared a lot about the extra penny. You might not believe this, but a penny – an old penny – was worth something then, that is, you noticed the difference between having it and not having it. I've seen my own kids lose a pound and not think about it as much as I thought about that extra penny. Eric was already holding it out on his palm in the flickering darkness – one penny and two threepenny bits. I took them and gave him the tooth in a hurry – I didn't want to miss any more of *Thunder Riders*.

'Your tooth's gone, then,' my mum said, when I came home and she saw the gap.

'I swallowed it,' I said, looking sad.

'Never mind,' she said, and I could see she was relieved that the tooth fairy hadn't got to fork out another sixpence. I'd lost two teeth the week before. They started coming out late but once they got going there was no holding them and my big brother Ted was still shedding the odd grinder. She gave me a penny, as a sort of consolation prize, so I was tuppence up on that tooth. I didn't tell her about flogging it to Eric Donnelly for sevenpence. She'd have thought it was a bit odd. I thought it was a bit odd myself.

It was half-term that weekend so I didn't see Eric till we were back at school on Wednesday. Yes, Wednesday. Half-terms were short, then, like everything else: trousers, money ... He was round the back of the bog with Brian Ferris.

'Listen,' Eric was saying, 'threepence, then.'

'Nah,' said Brian, 'I want to keep it.'

'But you said your mum didn't believe in the tooth fairy,' Eric persisted. 'You been losing teeth for two years for *nothing*! If you let me have it you'll get threepence – *four*pence.'

'I want it,' said Brian. 'I want to keep it in a box and watch it go rotten.'

'Fivepence,' said Eric.

'It's mine. I want it.' Brian walked away and Eric retired defeated, but at dinner time I caught him at it again with Mary Arnold, over by the railings.

'How much does your tooth fairy give you?' he asked.

'A shilling,' said Mary, smugly.

'No deal, then,' Eric said, shrugging.

'But I'll let *you* have it for thixpenth,' said Mary, and smiled coyly. She always was soft, that Mary.

I started to keep an eye on Eric after that, him and his collection. It wasn't *what* he was collecting that was strange – Tony Mulholland collected bottle tops – it was the fact that he was prepared to pay. I noticed several things. First, the size of the tooth had nothing to do with the amount that Eric would cough up. A socking great molar might go for a penny, while a little worn-down bottom incisor would change hands at sixpence or sevenpence. Also, that he would never go above elevenpence. That was his ceiling. No one ever got a shilling out of Eric Donnelly, even for a great big thing with roots. Charlie McEvoy had one pulled by the dentist and brought it to school for Eric but Eric only gave him sevenpence for it.

'Here, Charlie,' I said, at break. 'What's he do with them?'

'Search me,' said Charlie, 'he's had three of mine.'

'D'you have a tooth fairy at home?' I was beginning to smell a rat.

'Yes,' said Charlie. 'Let's go and beat up

Ferris.' He was a hard man, was McEvoy; started early. He's doing ten years for GBH right now, and the Mulhollands are waiting for him when he comes out.

'No – hang about. How much?'

'Sixpence.' I was quite surprised. I wouldn't have put it past old McEvoy to keep a blunt instrument under the pillow, bean the tooth fairy and swipe the night's takings. He was a big fellow, even at eight. I wasn't quite so big, but Eric, although he was a year older, was smaller than me. That day I followed him home.

It was not easy to follow Eric home. They tended to marry early in that family so Eric not only had a full set of grandparents but also two great-grandmothers and enough aunties to upset the national average. As his mum seemed to have a baby about every six months Eric was always going to stay with one of them or another. He was heading for one of his great-grandmas that evening, along Jubilee Crescent. I nailed him down by the phone box.

'Listen, Donnelly,' I said. 'What are you doing with all them teeth?'

Give him credit, he didn't turn a hair. A lot of kids would have got scared, but not Eric. He just said, 'You got one for me, then?'

'Well, no,' I said, 'but I might have by Saturday.'

'Sevenpence?' said Eric, remembering the

previous transaction, I suppose. He had a head for figures.

'Maybe,' I said, 'but I want to know what you do with them.'

'What if I won't tell you?' Eric said.

'I'll knock all yours out,' I suggested, so he told me. As I thought, it was all down to the grannies and aunties. They were sorry for poor little Eric – Dad out of work, all those brothers and sisters and no pocket money. If he lost a tooth while he was staying with one of them he put it under the pillow and the tooth fairy paid up. There being two great-grannies, two grannies and seven aunties, it was hard for anyone to keep tabs on the number of teeth Eric lost and it hadn't taken him long to work out that if he didn't overdo things he could keep his eleven tooth fairies in business for years. Kids who didn't have a tooth fairy of their own were happy to flog him a fang for a penny. If he had to pay more than sixpence the tooth went to Great-Granny Ennis, who had more potatoes than the rest of them put together.

By the time that he was eleven I calculate that Eric Donnelly had lost one hundred teeth, which is approximately twice as many as most of us manage to lose in a lifetime. With the money he saved he bought a second-hand barrow and toured the streets touting for scrap, returnable bottles and so on, which was what earned him enough to buy the two hundred and fifty Victorian baths with claw feet which is the beginning of the public part of Eric's success story, where we came in. I suppose there is some justice in the fact that at thirty-eight Eric no longer has a single tooth he can call his own.

No – I am not Eric's dentist. I am his dustman, and I sometimes catch a glimpse of the old cushion grips as I empty the bin. Occasionally I turn up just as Eric is leaving for a board meeting. He flashes his dentures at me in a nervous grin and I give him a cheery wave like honest dustmen are meant to do.

'Morning, Donnelly,' I shout merrily. 'Bought any good teeth lately?' He hates that.

Dan, Dan, the Scenery Man

The first time June saw Dad on stage she was only six and she did not recognize him. The play had been about Noah's Ark and June had gone along with Mum hoping to see the animals come in two by two. Instead it was just people in bedspreads who spent most of their time sitting round a table, arguing. Dad turned up in the middle of one fierce row as a bent old man wearing a thin white beard, and even when Mum nudged her and hissed, 'There's Daddy,' June could hardly believe it. They went home straight after the performance and Dad came in about an hour later, tall, upright, young again, but his chin looked red and sore where the beard had come off.

The village dramatic society staged a pantomime every Christmas. This year it was *Dick Whittington*. Dad never really acted, he said he preferred to be backstage, and still only appeared in what he called 'walk-on parts' in which he did just that; walked on and later walked off again. But he went to the village hall every Friday evening and at weekends disappeared into the garden shed where he built

London Bridge and the Sultan's palace out of hardboard. His friend Simon, who was playing Alderman Fitzwarren, came along to help and in between sawing and hammering, Dad heard his lines. Sometimes Simon broke into song, ditties about diddling and fiddling and financial scandals. Mum said she supposed it would sound funny on the night.

'Why don't you join the society?' June asked her. Dad had abandoned that suggestion long ago.

'I've got something better to do with my time,' Mum said, regularly. She always did the ironing on Friday nights, as if to prove that she had no time for play-acting. 'Anyway,' she added, 'I can't act.'

'Nor can most of them,' June said. She did a lot of drama at school these days, and knew that there was more to acting than pretending to be somebody else. You had to turn yourself into somebody else, be them and think for them, even if it were for only a few minutes at a time. The society members looked impressive on stage, very at-home and confident, but watching from the dark of the village hall she could never forget that they were Mr Sleaman the dentist, Mrs Elsenham who ran the Cub Scouts, the estate agent, Simon from up the road. Very few of them could disappear inside someone else's skin as soon as they stepped out from the wings.

Mrs Elsenham played pretty young girls, but you never lost sight of Mrs Elsenham who was pretty, but not a girl, and rather gathered about the neck, like a draw-string bag. In the pantomine she was Alderman Fitzwarren's daughter Alice.

'Simon's *daughter*?' Mum said, when Dad told them. 'She's old enough to be his mother!'

'Sister,' Dad protested, mildly. Mum was at that moment very busy with housework, as she always was when Dad mentioned the dramatic society. But June loved hearing about rehearsals. She longed to join the society herself when she was old enough. Children were sometimes borrowed for special occasions, particularly the pantomimes, when fairies or small animals were required. This year there was to be a rat ballet, which danced about teasing Dick Whittington's cat. June had known better than to ask if she could audition for it. Dad would have liked her to.

She was in bed when he came home from rehearsals, although she always heard him slam the front gate. Anything he wanted to tell her had to wait till breakfast next day, so it was one Saturday morning, at the beginning of December, when he came into the kitchen and said, 'We've got a bit of a crisis on our hands.'

'What's a crisis?' June asked. 'Like on the news?'

'It means the Good Fairy has developed a septic toe,' Mum said grimly.

'We don't have a Good Fairy in *Dick Whittington*,' Dad said.

'It was a septic toe last year. Anyone would think her leg had dropped off, the fuss you all made.'

'Well, she did have a lot of dancing to do. No, we've actually *lost* a dancer, this time.'

'Went down the plughole, I suppose.'

'The Malones are going away for Christmas.'

'I didn't think they belonged.' Mr and Mrs Malone sang in the choral society, in evening dress. It was hard to imagine them banging about at the village hall wearing false beards and fishnet tights.

'They don't, but little Zara belongs to the dancing class and she was our solo rat. She does – did – a dance in front of the curtain while the senior rats do a quick change into belly-dancers for scene three.'

'That's a crisis,' Mum said to June, witheringly.

'What I thought was ...' Dad said, and then he seemed to think again. 'You're doing Christmas things at school now, aren't you? Not much work?'

June nodded. They were right in the middle of that lovely break-down in routine that went on until they broke up; post boxes, decorations, carols in assembly, the Nativity Play, in which she, like Dad, had a walk-on part; always a shepherd, never the Virgin Mary.

'What's all this?' Mum's mouth went tight and suspicious. Nativity Plays were all right, unavoidable even. Everyone had them, like Income Tax demands, but they both knew that Dad had something else in mind.

'I was thinking of that butterfly dance you did at the school concert. You could still do it, couldn't you? You haven't forgotten it?'

'A butterfly instead of a rat?' June said.

Mum said, 'Dick Whittington's cat didn't hunt butterflies, come off it, Keith.'

'The same dance, only dressed as a rat – the costume Zara wears would fit you. And, as I recall, it might just as well have been a rat last time, except for the wings. Not that it wasn't very nice,' he added, hurriedly, 'but it wasn't all that much like butterflies.'

'You mean, I could be in the panto and go to rehearsals?' She spoke to Dad but she looked at Mum.

'And come home at half-past eleven?' Mum said. 'Don't be silly.'

'We'd come straight home at ten,' Dad said. 'And there's only a couple more evening rehearsals before she breaks up; *Friday* evenings … no falling asleep in class.'

'It's not to become a habit,' Mum said.

'How could it?'

'Not a regular thing—'

'A one-off. Promise.' If only he wouldn't wheedle. 'I just thought it might be fun for her.'

Half the fun was in looking forward to it, spreading the news at school, telling snooty Zara Malone that she would be stepping into her role.

'You're welcome,' Zara informed her. 'I didn't want to be a rat anyway. You wait till you put that smelly old mask on.'

'I have,' June said. She had tried out the costume the night before. 'It smells of you. *Eau de Malone*. Yuk!' They were separated by the headmaster before June could return Zara's kick. Her ankle was sore all day but she was too pleased with the *Eau de Malone* crack to care.

Rehearsals began at seven-thirty. At seven o'clock it was already a stone-cold night, still, silent, beaded with stars, as June and Dad walked over the level crossing, through the council estate and up the hill to the village hall. From far away they could see the three long windows shining warmly like lanterns above the houses.

Once inside, away from the black night, the icy stars, June noticed how thin and chill the light really was, how the air smelled of dust and cigarette smoke, but the magic was working already. At one end of the hall was the stage, a box filled with golden glow, and on it Dad's scenery, no longer bits of deal and hardboard but Highgate Hill, where Dick heard the bells of London calling him back to become Lord Mayor; and there was the milestone where he sat to rest, and beyond it the backdrop; London as it must have looked hundreds of years ago; red roofs and steeples gathered round the high dome of St Paul's, and never a tower block in sight. Beside the milestone, sleeves rolled up, a clipboard under his arm, stood Mr Sleaman, the dentist. Without his white smock he looked wild and unreliable as he ran his fingers through his hair and made furious gestures to the Vicar who was up a step-ladder at the side of the hall, wrestling with a spotlight. When he saw Dad he waved his flailing arms and called, 'Hello, Dan! What do you think of it?'

Dad waved back. 'Great stuff, Tom, though I say it myself!' Mr Sleaman's name really was Tom, but Dad was called Keith. June was just about to ask him why he answered to Dan, but he gently shunted her forward. 'Tom, meet our replacement rat.'

Mr Sleaman vaulted lightly down from the stage, rushed over to June, shook her hand, cried madly that she was an angel, and swarmed up the ladder where he collided with the Vicar who was swarming down, like a pirate descending from the rigging with a spanner in his teeth.

'If I were you,' Dad said, 'I'd just sit down somewhere quietly and watch until we call you.'

He flung off his duffle-coat, pushed up his sleeves and dived through a door at the side of the stage.

A voice on the other side of it shrieked, 'Dan! Darling! *When* are you going to fix this flat? It simply *flaps* every time I open the window.' June knew the voice. She had last heard it at that volume in July, at the village fête, marshalling Cub Scouts for a gymnastic display. Dad bobbed out from behind a tree on the stage.

'Have no fear, Dan is here,' he hollered, whipping out a screwdriver. June gazed. What was the matter with him?

All round her people were taking off coats and unwinding scarves to pile on the stacking chairs that lined the sides of the hall. Every few seconds a blast of cold air scoured her legs as someone flounced in from the darkness and dragged the door shut. No one walked or spoke. They skipped, dodged, hit each other on the back, while laughing, shouting, squealing. Six woman-sized girls from the dancing class – the ones who were doubling as rats and belly-dancers – slipped off their coats to reveal hairy body stockings, and began to limber up, swinging their legs dangerously. On all sides people called for Tom, the director, Sparks – who was the Vicar –

or Dan – who was Dad. Everyone wanted Dan. Mrs Elsenham was struck on the chin by the soaring hind leg of a belly-dancing rat. June heard the Vicar say damn, twice.

At half-past seven, when the rehearsal was due to begin, they all looked as if they had been there for hours. Tom danced into the middle of the mob and clapped his hands. 'All right, troupers! Let's start with a quick run-through of scenes two and three so we can see how our new little rat shapes up.' He made a magnificent gesture in June's direction. Every head turned toward her and people clapped.

'Dan's girl,' a voice said.

'Does her mother know she's out?' said another. Both voices laughed and June felt uneasy, but after a moment there was a kind of restless hush and on to the stage walked Dad's mate Simon. He turned to the front, rubbed his hands and said, 'Just off to the Stock Exchange. I think I'll put in a spot of insider-dealing before lunch.' There was something odd about Simon. June saw him often enough in the shed, with Dad, and he always had a part in the plays – but he didn't quite seem to be acting. On the other hand, he wasn't the nice, ordinary Simon who came round on Saturdays, any more than the Vicar seemed to be the Vicar, or Mrs Elsenham, the cub mistress. And if June had never seen Tom Sleaman before, she would not have dreamed of allowing him anywhere near her teeth.

Mrs Elsenham was, without doubt, the battiest of the lot, tripping about with a floaty scarf that snagged on the scenery so that 'Darling Tom' or 'Darling Simon' or 'Darling Dan' had to rush on stage and unhook her. Dan was everywhere, efficient, dependable Dan. Each time somebody fussed or complained – Mrs Elsenham was in tears at one point and wailed that she could not go on – Tom Sleaman or the Vicar would say, 'Dan will see to it ... Make a note of that, Dan,' and the fuss would subside.

The rat solo was a success, no one could have guessed that it had started out as a butterfly. As June appeared on stage alone – while the other rats changed into belly-dancers, swapping their tails and whiskers for harem pants and spangled bras – there was no need to rehearse with anyone else except Dick Whittington's cat who worked at the estate agent's and came creeping round the curtains at the end to chase her into the wings. People applauded kindly and Mrs Elsenham, lurking backstage, swatted her with a damp kiss and said she was a natural. June supposed that was a compliment.

The rehearsal ran late and it was almost ten before June and Dad got away. The others were straggling off to the Black Prince, for a post mortem, they said, which June had thought was something you did with corpses.

'Don't you want to go with them?' June said. Now she understood why Dad came home at eleven-thirty on Fridays.

'Not tonight,' he said, and tucked her arm into his. 'I'm seeing my girl home.'

They walked down the hill where the pavements glittered with frost.

'Dad?'

'Mmm?'

'Why do they call you Dan?'

'It started as a joke,' he said. 'Somebody called

me Dan, Dan, the Scenery Man, and it stuck.'

She said, 'Is that why you pretend ...?' and tailed off, not quite sure what she had meant to ask.

'I don't pretend.'

'But you aren't like that really.'

'What do you mean by really?' Dad said. 'Think what I do for a living: sell shoes. I don't have to be Dan, Dan, the Scenery Man in Dolcis, do I? I couldn't be.'

'You aren't like that at home.'

'We don't need Dan at home, either,' Dad said. 'Your mum sees to all that.'

'Are you acting, then?'

'I can't act. If I could, I wouldn't be doing the scenery, would I?'

They walked on, through the council estate. There were already Christmas trees in some of the windows.

'But you were all being different, weren't you?'

'How long do you think Mrs E would last with the Cubs if she went on like that? We're just being ourselves,' he said, 'but you're right, in a way; different selves.'

'Like – acting being actors?'

'And electricians, and scenery men. Maybe Sparks really is an electrician, and only acts being a vicar. Acting isn't just pretending, is it?'

They had to wait at the level crossing for the

ten-twenty from Ashford to trundle into the station.

'Do you like being Dan, Dan, the Scenery Man?'

'Better than selling shoes, to tell the truth.'

June looked up at his face, lit in flashes from the passing train.

'Aren't you happy?' She pressed his arm. She had not thought before that he might not be.

'Not all the time. Are you?'

'No … not *happy*.'

'Of course not.' The crossing barriers rose slowly, like curtains swept aside. They moved forward. 'I can't say you'll grow out of it because you're just growing into it.'

'Into what?'

'Well …' He seemed unsure. 'Just growing up, really. You don't change, as you get older, but you learn to *seem* different when you need to, when you want to be.'

They were almost home. 'Mum doesn't,' June said. 'She's always the same.'

'How do you know? How do you know what she's like when you're not there – when she isn't being Mum. What do you think she's doing now?'

'Ironing,' June said, her hand on the gate.

'No – don't open it. Sssh! Wait.' Dad silently stepped over their low garden wall and beckoned June to follow. 'Walk on the grass,' he whispered. 'Now, come round to the side.'

The heavy brown curtains were drawn across the bay window of the living room, but the little side window was hung with net. June and Dad crept towards it and peered through. Inside Mum was sitting on the settee with her shoes off and her feet drawn up. The biscuit tin was open beside her, and a coffee cup was balanced on the arm of the settee; something she would never allow June to do for fear of spillage.

The television was on, through the glass they could hear lush romantic music. Dad looked down at June, raised his eyebrows and slipped away across the dark garden. A moment later she heard the gate open and then slam, and she ran round to the front to meet Dad as he crunched slowly up the gravel path.

When he opened the front door there was no sound of music from the telly; instead they heard the unmistakeable clang of the tubular steel ironing board being folded up in the kitchen. Mum came out to meet them with a stack of sheets in her arms.

'Have a good time?' she asked, wearily.

'June's a star in the making,' Dad said, and for a second she could almost hear Dan, Dan, the Scenery Man. 'Look, you sit down. We'll make some coffee. Put the kettle on, Rat Woman!'

June went into the kitchen. The biscuit tin stood on the working surface, beside the iron, and the coffee cup was draining on the washing-up rack. As she stood, waiting for the kettle to boil, she touched her finger to the iron. It was quite cold.

Mystery Tour

'Do you want the good news first, or the bad news?' says Fig, on the telephone. And then, before I can answer, goes on, 'or the worse news, or the very worst?'

'The bad,' I said, and added quickly, 'then the good,' because if I let Fig run on to the worse news and then the worst, I might not be in any condition to enjoy the good news.

'OK,' Fig said, sounding just like the man at the station who cancels trains. 'Mum can't take us to London next week. She's got an interview.'

'Oh,' I said. I felt as though I'd known that would happen all along. After *my* mum refused to let me go to London with Fig alone and unsupervised – those were the words she used – it seemed too good to be true when Fig's mum said that she would take us. I'd been right. It was too good to be true.

'What's the good news, then?'

'My Auntie Cathy will take us instead.'

I'd seen Fig's Auntie Cathy once or twice. 'That's the *good* news?'

'It's better than not going at all,' Fig said; 'I think.'

'What's the worse news?'

'She can't drive. We're going by coach.'

'That's not the end of the world.'

'And she's bringing Damian too.'

'That's the end of the world.' Damian is Fig's cousin. He is four years old. He whines for England.

'Can't she get a babysitter?'

'She says it's time Damian went to London.'

'Why? What's London done?'

Fig and I had planned to go to London to visit the Science Museum. Fig's mum had said that was fine by her, she'd go to the V&A next door and meet us afterwards. Auntie Cathy, as it turned out, had other ideas.

'She says it's a pity to go all that way just for one museum,' Fig reported, next morning. 'She says we ought to go early and make a proper day of it.'

'Doing what?'

'Dunno,' Fig said, gloomily. 'She's got something lined up. She says we'll find out when we get there.'

'Magical mystery tour?'

'Tragical history tour,' Fig said.

Mum got me up at *six* on Friday morning, so I could leave at seven-fifteen to meet Fig and Auntie Cathy and Damian at the bus stop in time to catch the seven-forty coach. As I came round the corner into the main road I saw them standing in a row at the end of the queue and it was clear, from the way they were standing, that there had already been a row of some sort.

When they saw me coming Fig switched on a heavy scowl as an early warning, but Auntie Cathy whipped a shiny smile into place. Damian, who looked like a dwarf Sumo wrestler in green Bermuda shorts, was head-butting a nearby litter bin.

'You must be Ozzie,' says Auntie Cathy, which made me want to say why must I be? But before I got the chance the coach drew up and Auntie Cathy, who had seemed daft but steady up to that point, if you see what I mean, began flapping. She's the sort of woman who looks as though she's been put together out of string. Everything she wore had loops and knots and fringes on it. Even her hair looked like that fuzzy tuft you get on macramé plant-pot holders. When she flapped, all the loose ends flapped too.

'Oh my goodness, you cut that fine, didn't you, we might have missed it, oh—'

'It's early,' Fig growled. 'Anyway, they go every twenty minutes.'

'I think it's the seven-twenty running late, actually,' I said. I don't like bossy grown-ups, but I can't stand bossy grown-ups who know less than I do. They make me go stiff and grind my teeth. I had a timetable too, and she didn't. And now she was wound up she began to spin. She had an enormous string tote-bag hung on her shoulder and she was scrabbling about in it, up to the elbows, like churning. Things started coming to the top – tissues, apples, books, freezer boxes, bottles. The queue was moving away from us. Fig managed to steer her towards the door of the coach by walking forwards until she had to step backwards, but by the time we were at the head of the queue she was still head-first in the tote-bag.

'You haven't lost your purse again, have you?' Fig hopped on to the coach and hung out of the doorway in case the driver got fed up and left without us. All along the side of the coach you could see irritated faces pressed against the windows, wondering what the hold-up was. They weren't any more irritated than me, I can tell you.

'It's in here somewhere,' Auntie was blathering.

'I want to go home.' That was Damian. 'I don't like queues. I want to watch television.' He started kicking the coach.

'I've got a tenner,' said Fig, getting desperate. 'What about you, Oz?'

'So've I.' I waved the note urgently under Auntie Cathy's nose. 'Twenty pounds'll pay for one and two halves. Under-fives are free.'

'Are you thinking of coming with us?' the

driver asked. Inside the coach the other passengers were starting to mutter. People use these early coaches to get to work on. They don't think much of day-trippers, especially batty day-trippers. Someone said, 'Ever travelled by coach before, lady?'

'I'll go to a cash-till when we get to London,' Auntie promised. 'I'll pay you back then. I've got my purse in here somewhere, but – Oh, one and two halves, please, driver, so sorry – I put the money for the fares on the hall table, so as to remember it on the way out – no, that one's under five …'

The coach was full and we could not sit together – fortunately. Fig and I were one behind the other at the back and Auntie Cathy was in the middle, with Damian on her lap; near enough, though, for us to be able to hear Damian.

'I want to sit by the window. Why can't I sit by the window? I want to go home. I feel sick. I want to go to the toilet. *Why* can't I sit next to the window? I want to watch television.' In the end it just became a sort of high-pitched noise in the background: 'Iyiyiyiyiyiyiyiyyyyyyyyyy …'

'Does he go on like that all the time?' I asked Fig. I had to lean forwards and sideways because Fig was in the seat ahead of me.

'Yes, but can you blame him?' Fig said, over his shoulder. 'He didn't want to come, anyway. And she's turned the whole day upside down because of him.'

I was alarmed. 'Why? Aren't we going to the Science Museum, then?'

'Yes, but we're going somewhere else as well, first.'

'Where?'

'She won't tell me. It's supposed to be a lovely surprise.'

'I hate surprises,' I said. 'I like to know what's going on.' And without the ten pounds I felt unprotected. So long as you've got money with you, you feel there's a way out. Without it you feel trapped, you're at other people's mercy. Grown-ups never seem to realize that, though you'd think they'd feel it more than we do.

'Well, we're having a picnic somewhere, if it doesn't rain. That was meant to be a secret too, but Damian was digging around in the bag and found the sandwich boxes.'

Damian's voice rose up to new heights. 'I don't want to go to London. I don't want to sit on your lap. I want to look out of the window.'

'If it goes any higher,' I said hopefully, 'we won't be able to hear him at all. Like a bat.'

We waited for that to happen, but it didn't, so we spent the rest of the journey working out ways to lose Damian in London. Most of them were quite cruel, involving escalators and live rails, but we couldn't plan anything in detail because we didn't know where we were going. I don't really mind surprises, so long as I don't know they're going to happen until they do happen, if you see what I mean. What I can't stand are surprises that you are expecting, the kind that you can see creeping up on you, like this one. Because with Auntie Cathy's kind of surprise you have plenty of time to imagine what it might turn out to be, and to be afraid that it will be a disappointment when it does happen. Or a disaster. Fig and I were fairly sure that we wouldn't enjoy anything that Auntie Cathy might spring on us.

Also, we didn't have a lot of faith in Auntie Cathy at all, what with her bringing Damian and *not* bringing enough money. Fig said he thought the best thing of all would be losing both of them.

'But not till she's been to the bank,' I said. 'When we've got our money back, we'll lose them.'

We were joking, of course.

And we didn't get our money back.

When the coach got to Baker Street, *really* into the traffic jams, Fig waded up the aisle to ask Auntie Cathy where we'd be getting off. When he came back he didn't look too pleased.

'Don't tell me,' I said. 'It's a surprise.'

'No – she says we'll go on to Victoria Station if the traffic's clear down Park Lane, but if it isn't we'll get off at Marble Arch. She says she knows an alternative route. She's got the tube map out.'

'At least she's got a map,' I said. 'You can't go wrong with a tube map. It's got names on. It isn't just X marks the spot.'

'Look here,' Fig said, bitterly, 'she got lost coming to the bus stop. *That* was an alternative route. We only got there a couple of minutes before you did.'

'And then she complained that *I* was late,' I said. I saw then that if anything did go wrong today, it would be our fault, even if we didn't lose Auntie Cathy or push Damian under a train.

Things started to go wrong at Marble Arch. OK, blame the traffic. If we'd gone on to Victoria *none* of it would have happened, but it took twenty minutes to get from Baker Street to Marble Arch – on the coach. You can walk it in ten. And so we all piled out. This time Damian wanted to stay *on* the coach because he could see that now there were lots of empty seats next to windows, but Fig kind of lifted him down the steps on the toe of his trainer – no, it wasn't a kick – without Auntie Cathy seeing, and we headed back up the road to the tube station.

'Hang about,' said Fig, running on ahead to the corner, 'I can see a bank – hint, hint,' so we went down Oxford Street to the bank, which was quite a long way down, but when we got there it was shut because it wasn't nine-thirty yet. Auntie Cathy zoomed towards the hole in the wall, waving her cash card. Out came some money – after she'd punched in the wrong number and then asked for a new cheque book instead of cash.

What we didn't realize, until it was too late, was that the hole in the wall only had twenty-pound notes in it, so Fig and I didn't get our tenners back.

'Don't worry, I'll get change at the station,' Auntie Cathy trilled; so we trekked back to Marble Arch and down the steps to the underground.

More trouble; Damian didn't like it. Well, I didn't like it myself. Marble Arch underground station can't be anybody's favourite place, but I didn't go blue in the face and start screaming, even when Auntie still didn't give us our dosh, though I felt like it. He didn't like the crowds and he didn't like the queue at the ticket window, but what he didn't like most of all was a sort of eerie yoo-hooing that came yodelling up the escalator and, really, it was a bit like something out of *An American Werewolf in London*, but we did think he might stop when we explained that it was only a busker. He didn't. It turned out he didn't know what a busker was and by the time we got to the bottom of the escalator he was practically trying to climb back up it again. Still, at least he could see it was only a hairy dude with a guitar, singing *On Blue Bayou*.

We still hadn't got our money back, though.

At least we had our tickets. Auntie had had to give us those to get through the automatic gates. Hooray for automatic gates. If it hadn't been for the tickets we might still be going round and round.

You turn right at the bottom of the escalator at Marble Arch, and there is a staircase down to the lines, which run east and west, with a passage between the platforms. We could hear a train roaring down there and a terrific draft came up that set all of Auntie Cathy's fringes flapping. We were halfway down the stairs while she was still peeling Damian off the escalator and dragging him past the werewolf, so by the time she caught us up the train had gone.

'Was it eastbound or westbound?' Auntie said.

'West.'

Fig was scowling again but Auntie Cathy gave a light laugh.

'Not to worry. We'll get an eastbound train instead.'

'Change of plan?' I said, innocently, but she wasn't falling for that.

'Never you mind. We'll get there soon enough.'

That started Damian off again. '*Where* are we

going? Are we lost? I don't like it here. I want to go to the toilet.'

There was an eastbound train due in two minutes, which gave Auntie Cathy time to nip along the platform and check out the big tube map on the wall. We scooted after her to see if we could guess what she was up to, but she just did squiggly movements with one finger, like the map was in Braille, that took in half a dozen stations. She could have been pointing at anywhere.

'Oh, that's fine,' she said. 'We'll change at Bond Street, on to the Jubilee Line, and then change again—'

'What's a jublyline? I don't want a jublyline.' Damian. 'I want to go to the park.'

'We *are* going to the park – well, it's a sort of park,' Auntie said, cautiously. 'Oh, look, here's the train.'

It was packed, that train. It was like those pictures you see of the Tokyo underground where they've got people specially employed to push the passengers on board until the doors shut. Only we had to get ourselves on, and we were all squashed together in one corner, up against the fire extinguisher. Damian was starting to go purple, with rage or oxygen starvation.

'I want to go to the park. I want to see ducks.'

'We'll see ducks, darling.'

'I want to see aeroplanes.'

'I expect we'll see aeroplanes. Yes, I'm sure we will.'

Fig leaned over and said, man to man – well, man to auntie – 'Look, where *are* we going, exactly?'

'Ask no questions and I'll tell you no lies,' Auntie Cathy twittered.

'We are going to the museum, aren't we?' I said, trying to look tearful. I nearly was, too. With fury.

'Of course we are – *afterwards*. Here we are. Out we get. All stick together!' She made everything sound like PE at first school.

Half the passengers seemed to get out at Bond Street and we were swept along the platform towards the sign that pointed to the Jubilee Line. It was all we could do to stick together, but you could always tell where Damian was. I had him in my earhole all the way. 'Where's the park? Where's the ducks? Where's the aeroplanes?'

Then we got sucked into a whirlpool of people at the bottom of the escalator and suddenly, as we shot out on to the platform, Damian's voice was coming from up ahead.

'I don't want to go on another train. I want to see the aeroplanes. *Where* are we going?'

'Oh, be quiet!'

I looked round at Fig. He raised his eyebrows. Even Auntie Cathy had had enough.

The Jubilee Line platform was emptier; there were only about a hundred people on it instead of five thousand, and there was room to breathe. It was the southbound platform, so I suppose most people were heading the other way, for the middle of London. Fig and I went straight to the wall map to see if we could guess where we were going, when Damian let rip again.

'Where are we going? I don't like this. Where are we going?'

'Wait and see,' Auntie Cathy said, but she was weakening, I could tell, and Damian could tell, too. He knew just how to handle her. Fig and I had been too restrained.

'Where are we *going*?'

Suddenly Auntie Cathy's fringes started floating again and I heard the train approaching. And I also heard her say, 'Oh, for heaven's sake! First of all we're going to queue for the picnic—'

'I don't want to queue,' Damian howled. 'I want to go to the park. Why—'

And then the train roared in. I'm not sure what happened next, but Auntie Cathy and Damian were nearer to the edge of the platform than we were. This train was packed too, and as the doors opened a great mob of people surged out, and Damian and Auntie Cathy disappeared. Fig and I fought our way towards the nearest door, but just as we were about to get on, some more idiots who'd been stuck in the middle of the carriage came thundering out and we got swept back again, and before we could do anything the doors had shut and the train had started.

We just stood there. People were barging round us and shoving, and then there was no one, just us, and the last carriage of the train sliding past, towards the tunnel. And we'd both seen the same thing – Auntie Cathy hadn't noticed. When the doors closed she was still squawking at Damian who was still squawking at her. I turned to Fig.

'What will she do?'

'How should I know?'

'I mean, will she come back for us or will she wait for us to catch up?'

'How can we catch up? We don't know where she's going.'

'She said we'd have to change again.'

'I know, but she didn't say where.'

'She started to tell Damian, something about queuing for a picnic, but I didn't hear all of it.' If only he'd worn her down faster!

I tried to stay calm. Ever since I was tiny and started going places with Mum, she's always said the same thing: 'If we get separated, stay put. I'll come back for you.' I somehow didn't think that Auntie Cathy would do anything that sensible.

'She's bound to notice in a minute,' Fig said. 'We'd better stay here.'

So we sat down on those funny little seats that stick out of the wall like plastic laps. Another train came in. I looked at my watch: ten minutes. Then Fig said, 'She'll be on the other line, won't she? This is the southbound. Northbound's across the hall.'

'But she'll know we're here, won't she?'

'Why hasn't she come back, then? She must be waiting for us.'

'Where?'

But, just in case, we crossed the hall to the northbound platform and went to study the wall map while we waited. 'Look,' Fig said, 'there's only two places where you can change on the Jubilee, south of here: Green Park and Westminster. Then it goes to Waterloo. If she wanted to go to Waterloo we'd have got off the coach at Baker Street.'

'So where were we supposed to be going when we did change?' That was the trouble, there were so many lines. At Green Park you can change on to the Piccadilly and the Victoria. Westminster is for the District and Circle.'

'Maybe it was Green Park,' Fig said. 'She did say it was a sort of park we were going to.'

'Green Park's a real park,' I said, 'not a sort of anything. And we were going to change, not get out.'

'She said there'd be aeroplanes. Where would we go to see aeroplanes?'

I was looking at my watch again: twenty minutes, now. I was starting to get really worried. Surely the silly bat had realized that we didn't know where she was and would come back for us. Then it struck me that since we'd crossed to the northbound platform, there hadn't been any trains for her to come back on, and at the same moment there was a kind of booming explosion overhead and a voice said, 'Good morning, ladies and gentlemen; this is your Jubilee Line information service. Owing to a defective train at Green Park, all services on this line will be subject to delay and cancellation.' And then there was a lot more about going round by Oxford Circus to Baker Street. So that was why Auntie Cathy hadn't come back; the line was blocked.

'We'll have to go after her,' I said.

'Yes, but *where*?' We seemed to take turns to say this.

'If she's not at Green Park she'll be at Westminster.' I tried to sound confident.

'Yes, but supposing she knows about the defective train? Maybe *she's* coming back via Oxford Circus.'

'Maybe she's on the defective train.'

We were beginning to realize what a mess we were in, because in losing Auntie Cathy we'd lost everything else: coach tickets, money, food ... all we had were our underground tickets. We were all right so long as we stayed underground. We'd checked them right away to see if they had the destination on, but it only said where we'd come from, Marble Arch, and they were singles, so as soon as we went through a barrier we'd be stuck, penniless, somewhere in London. And neither of us knows London well – that's the trouble with the tube map. It makes you think you know where you are, only London isn't the same shape as the map.

'Let's go to Green Park,' Fig said. 'Even if she did get as far as Westminster before she missed us, she'd have got as far as Green Park coming back.' So we nipped across the hall again and there was a southbound train coming in. It wasn't so crowded as the other one but we didn't sit down. We stood by the doors and peered out as if we might see Auntie Cathy and Damian slogging back through the tunnel, but all we did see were those strange pipes that wiggle along the tunnel walls, and when we got to Green Park – they weren't there, either.

It was getting serious. We were trapped.

'Haven't you got *any* money?' I asked Fig. He looked in all his pockets.

'Twenty p. We could ring home.'

'When will your mum be in? Mine's out till five.'

'Six,' Fig said. 'She had to go to Birmingham – for that interview.'

We tried to decide which would be worse: pounding the streets of London all day or lurking in the bowels of the earth.

'Let's find a map again and try to work this out,' I said.

We found another map, with about fifteen gibbering tourists round it, but at last they cleared off and we closed in.

'Right,' Fig said, 'aeroplanes. Where are there aeroplanes?'

'Hendon,' I said, 'the aircraft museum.' After a long search we found Hendon, up near the top of the Northern Line.

'Couldn't be Hendon, then,' Fig said, 'otherwise we'd have gone north at Bond Street.'

'Maybe she was going to get the Northern Line at Waterloo.'

'But it would have been easier to stay on the Central and change at Tottenham Court Road – and quicker.'

'What about the Imperial War Museum, then – that's got aeroplanes.'

'Where do we get out for that?'

'Lambeth – that's on the Bakerloo. No, you were right, we'd have got off at Baker Street.'

'Or stayed on the Central till Oxford Circus,' Fig said. 'What about Docklands? That's got an airport.'

'It's not on the underground, though,' I said. 'It's got its own railway.'

'Where?'

'I don't know,' I snapped. 'Docklands is the East End, isn't it?'

'Hang about,' Fig said, 'they're *all* in the east, aren't they?'

'Hendon's not,' I said.

'East*ish*. Easter than Marble Arch. Don't you remember, when we got down the escalator at Marble Arch we were after a westbound train and we missed it?'

I did remember. 'That's right, and she said it didn't matter because we could get an eastbound and change at Bond Street. But we were *heading* west, we were meant to be.'

And we both looked at the left-hand edge of the map, and there, right at the end of the Piccadilly Line, where it turns back on itself, was a little picture of an aircraft, and we both said, at the same moment, 'Heathrow!'

'Do you really think she'd take us all the way out to Heathrow?'

'We're on the Piccadilly Line here,' Fig said.

'It's a hell of a way,' I said. 'Suppose we go all the way out there and we've made a mistake?'

'How much does it cost? Suppose we get out there and we've got the wrong tickets?'

I was still clutching my ticket and it was getting damp. I squinted at it again, in the hope that I might have missed something important the first time, but all it said was MARBLE ARCH C SINGLE 1.00, the date and lots of numbers.

'What's the C stand for?' Fig said.

'Child, I expect.'

'And the 1.00?'

'A pound?'

'Look,' Fig said, 'they're singles. How were we meant to get back?'

'By air?' I said, but Fig was past smiling.

'How can we get back?'

'Just hang on to the tickets,' I said. 'We're safe so long as we don't go through a barrier. We'll go to Heathrow, and if she's not there we'll come back here.'

'But it'll take so long,' Fig wailed, 'and there's two stations at Heathrow.'

'Let's start, anyway,' I said. 'You're right, it'll take ages. Maybe we'll have a better idea before we get there.'

We were just moving off to find the Piccadilly Line when Fig said, 'What's that?'

'What's what?'

'That other map.'

I hadn't noticed the other map, but it was on the wall next to the one we'd been looking at. All the tube lines were on it, but it was in patches of different colours, like contours: blue in the middle, then out through yellow, orange and so on. 'Zones', it said. Five of them.

Heathrow was in Zone Five.

I looked at the ticket again: 1.00. We'd never get to Heathrow for £1.

'Hendon's in Zone Three,' I said. 'Well, it's on the border.'

'But we weren't going north. What about Lambeth?'

'Zone One. We wouldn't have needed a £1 ticket for Zone One. Anyway, we weren't going east.'

Fig moaned and banged his head on the map. No one took any notice. No one had taken any notice of us at all. You wouldn't think you could feel so alone among so many people.

'Oz,' Fig pleaded, 'think again. Try and remember exactly what Auntie Cathy told Damian about what we were going to do.'

'I told you, I only heard a bit of it. She said we'd have to queue for the picnic first of all.'

'I don't get it,' Fig said. 'Why would we have to queue? She had the picnic in the bag.'

'Perhaps it was a special picnic place where you had to queue to get in.'

'Oh, come off it,' Fig said. 'You can picnic free all over London. There's the parks ... and the river ...'

'The river!' I said. 'Maybe we were going to come back by river. And look, if we were by the river we'd see the planes going into Heathrow.'

'Heathrow's in Zone Five.'

'Yes, but the Thames isn't. The Thames is in Two and Three, mostly. One even.'

We looked at the map again, and then Fig jumped, and grabbed my arm.

'*What* did she say?'

'When?'

'About the picnic.'

'That we'd be queuing for it.'

'Are you sure? Think. What did she say exactly?'

'I can't remember. Something like, "First of all we'll have to queue for the picnic" – no – "We're going to queue for—"'

Fig was grinning and stabbing at the map with his finger, near the river, at a station like Hendon, right on the edge of Zone Three: Kew Gardens.

'You dork!' Fig yelled. 'That's what she meant. We're going to Kew for the picnic – there you are. Kew. K-E-W. We can go on to Victoria and change to the District Line, or we can get the Piccadilly Line here and change at Earl's Court.'

We went via Victoria and got on a train to Richmond. Kew Gardens was the last station but one. It took us exactly twenty-nine-and-a-half minutes, which was less time than we'd spent hanging around between Bond Street and Green Park, but it felt like hours, because we weren't sure, up to the last minute, if we were right, and even if we were, it didn't mean that Auntie Cathy would be there, but she was. After Earl's Court the line's above ground, just like an ordinary railway, and there on the platform was Auntie Cathy, and Damian. Damian was crying and Auntie Cathy looked as if she had been. Even her fringes were all damp and droopy. When she saw us she leapt up and hugged Fig, and he didn't even struggle.

I thought we'd get a rocket, but even that didn't happen.

'It's all my fault,' Auntie Cathy kept saying, and I thought of asking for that in writing, but she really was crying now, with relief. 'I ought to have told you. I just kept praying that you'd overheard me telling Damian.'

'It's OK,' Fig said, patting her on the back, 'but we thought you'd come back for us.'

'I did,' Auntie Cathy sniffed, 'but the train got stuck so I came round by Oxford Circus and by the time I'd got back to Bond Street, you'd gone. How did you guess where we'd be?'

'Deduction,' Fig said, grandly. 'We worked it out by a process of elimination.'

He didn't let on that I'd half overheard her telling Damian where we were going, because that would have spoiled the effect. In fact it would have made us look as daft as she is, but Fig is a true friend and he didn't drop me in it. He didn't drop Auntie in it, either, when we got home. The whole thing is a horrid secret and I have changed names to protect the guilty.

Eye-opener

Mim was packing for school. It was hard work and Mim breathed heavily through her open mouth, spreading her possessions across the table among the toast crumbs and marmalade. On her knees lay the little yellow plastic briefcase that Gran had given her in September. Every item had to be inserted in a dozen different ways, like an awkward piece in a jigsaw puzzle, until Mim was satisfied and paused in her snuffling.

'An' *in* goes my itty book. An' *in* goes my itty horse. An' *in* goes my nice apple. An' *in* goes Long Jane Silver.'

Long Jane Silver was a Sindy doll with one leg. David had christened her in disgust but Mim, not understanding the joke, had thought it a lovely name and went on using it.

'Say bye-bye to Long Jane Silver,' Mim commanded them.

'Bye-bye, Long Jane Silver,' Mum said, with a teeny doll-sized wave.

'Bye-bye, Long Jane Silver,' Judy echoed. Judy was young enough to know better, David thought. *She* had no excuse for treating their little sister as a half-wit.

'Bye,' he said, through his teeth.

'Say, "Bye-bye, Long Jane Silver,"' Mim insisted, shoving the horrible thing under his nose.

'I said bye-bye.'

'You didn't say *proper* bye-bye,' Mim whimpered, in her little weak voice that made him want to strangle her. She knew exactly what he was thinking, too, and cringed convincingly.

'Just *say* it.' Mum glared at him.

'Look, how's she ever going to learn to speak properly if we all have to talk like her?' David said.

Mim was visibly crumpling, like a damp tissue. A tear trembled on her eyelashes as she cradled the doll, protectively. '*Poor* itty Long Jane Silver. *Poor* itty Long Jane Silver.'

'For God's sake, David!' His mother was beginning to smoulder at the edges. Getting everyone out of the house in the morning had become an exhausting ritual since Mim started school, attending the reception class in the mornings. The old routine involving dressing, eating, turns in the bathroom, perfected over the years, had broken down the minute that Mim had been allowed to believe that starting school was a major event.

All right, David conceded, it was a major event the *first* time. Mim turned it into a major event every morning.

'Poooooooor itty Long Jane Silver …'

'David!' Judy caught his eye, fiercely pleading. It was Judy who had to escort Mim to the infants' entrance before rushing round to join her own friends at the other end of the school.

'Bye-bye, Long Jane Silver.' David gave in. It was Judy, too, who had to bring her home again at noon instead of pitching into school lunch as she had always done before, because Mum could not get out of work before twelve-fifteen – as Mum reminded her every morning: 'Don't forget Mim at lunchtime.'

'But I can't today.' Judy looked appalled. The sky was falling. 'Mum, you know I can't.'

'Why not?' Now Mum too was looking thunderstruck. Well, of course; the Universe revolved around Mim.

'It's the play. We're going to the theatre – all the top forms. You gave me the money.'

'It's not today.'

'It is.'

'Next Thursday. I arranged to leave early *next* Thursday.'

'Well, it *is* today; the tenth. It *is*, Mum.' Now Judy was crumpling. Mim disintegrated entirely. Her mouth opened in an outraged roar.

'I CAN'T COME HOME FROM SCHOOL!'

'Hush, darling.' Mum soothed her flailing hair. 'Don't worry.' Mim continued to howl confidently. 'David will bring you home.'

'I can't,' David said, baldly.

'Of course you can.' Mim, crimson-faced, was holding her breath to see what happened. 'No one will mind if you come out a few minutes early. I'll write you a note.'

'It's not a few minutes. *We* don't finish till half-past twelve.'

'I'm sure they'll make an exception, just this once.'

'But it's games.'

'I'd have thought you'd want to come out early from games. You're always crabbing about it.' Judy, with Right on her side, could afford to look smug. She had parked herself in front of the calendar on the wall, with her finger resting thoughtfully on Thursday, 10 November, where it was written in red capitals: JUDY TO THEATRE.

'Yes, but I'll have to get changed—' He was cut short by a minor explosion. Mim, now purple, had finally choked. Judy flew to comfort her before Mum could move. Mum was already writing the note. Judy didn't want her to change her mind and David couldn't blame her for that. Judy loved looking after Mim and never complained about having to bring her home from school, but that was no reason why she should risk getting back too late to join the coach party and so miss the theatre trip.

As he cycled to school he overtook the two of

them, walking along the straight stretch by the railings, beyond which lay the primary school and, farther away still, his own, on the other side of the playing field. Usually he missed them altogether but because of the argument everyone was late out of the house this morning. Judy, he noticed, was trying to hurry, and Mim was dragging behind, limping piteously. The pavement was crowded with mothers towing Mim's classmates in the direction of the school, all going at a fair old lick however much the children whined and protested, but as David drew level Judy stopped, kneeled down in front of Mim, like a slave before an infant princess, and began retying her shoelaces. She did not see David as he pedalled past, but Mim did. He glanced back over his shoulder, and the expression on Mim's face could be described only as a smirk.

The memory of that smirk returned when he handed in his note at registration and was graciously given permission to leave school at eleven fifty, in order to get across to the infants' and collect his sister at twelve. There was nothing innocent about Mim's tyranny; she had them all just where she wanted them. On the day that Mum and Dad had returned from the maternity unit with Mim, almost five years ago, Elvis the cat, a far-sighted animal, had stormed out of the house in a jealous rage and stayed away for three days. Elvis had known what was coming. Now he lived mainly under the radiator in David's room, and Mim had taken his place as the family pet. That was the trouble; she wasn't being brought up as a future adult human, in fact, she was scarcely being brought up at all. Whatever might go on in the reception class during the morning, Mim went straight back to being a baby as soon as she came out of the door, aided and abetted by Dad, Mum, Judy, Gran – everyone except David and Elvis. Were they really the only ones who could see what was happening?

And then he forgot. He asked permission to leave games early, giving himself time to get changed before he set off across the field to the infants' block, but in the heat of the hockey game it went right out of his head until he saw Mr Flint gesturing at him from the edge of the pitch, waving and pointing at his watch.

David ran over to him, squelching in the cold mud. 'What's the time?'

'Ten to. Get your skates on.'

'I've got to go and change.'

'You won't have time. Get over there now.'

Mr Flint was right. The infants' block was much closer to the hockey pitch than his own school was. Some of the bigger infants were having a games lesson in their playground only a few metres away. By the time he had trekked back to the changing-room and returned it would be long after twelve.

'*Move*. I'll look after your stick ... head like a sieve ...' he heard Mr Flint mumbling, as he loped away in the direction of the low brick wall and high chain-link fence that cordoned off the infants from the huge and dangerous persons at the comprehensive. There was no gate in it and he had to trot all the way round the perimeter before he found a way into the building, but after all that he was still early. Mothers of ordinary infants were gathering outside in the street but, Judy had informed him, children in the reception class were picked up in the cloakroom, for safety's sake, and there were no mothers in there yet.

David, listening to the curious, high-pitched twittering made by twenty Mims in the classroom next door, sat down on a very low bench to wait. He felt like Gulliver in Lilliput, surrounded by midget wellingtons and mittens, tiny coats. Even sitting down, his chin was on a level with the coat hooks. Strangest of all was the row of miniature lavatories. He sat staring at them; surely *he* had never been this small?

There was a sound of water flushing and the door of the very last lavatory opened. Mim came out, straightening her skirt, and David, unnoticed, watched her with interest. Unaware that she was observed, this was a different Mim. She walked over to the washbasins, rose on tiptoe to reach the taps, rinsed her hands and dried them carefully on the roller towel. At home when she did this everybody was summoned to watch (until recently they had to admire her having a pee, too) accompanied by a broadcast commentary: 'Now Mim is washing her handses, like a good itty gir-ul. Here is the nice soap. Wash wash.' And lots of splashing which someone else had to wipe up.

Now she moved gravely round the cloakroom, frowning with concentration. For the first time in a long while David felt almost fond of her. He stood up.

'Hello, Mim.'

The effect was devastating. Mim swung round, rocking unsteadily, and gazed at him with large frightened eyes.

David, who had not meant to startle her, stepped forward, extending his hand. Mim let out a high, panicky wail, and fled in the direction of the classroom. David regretted his moment of weakness. She was a hopeless case, as bad here as she was at home, turning on the act as soon as she had an audience – and it was more of an audience than he had realized. In the last few minutes several mothers had joined him in the cloakroom, and were giving him funny looks, but these were nothing to the looks he was getting from the other direction. In the doorway of the classroom a small crowd of gawping, thumb-sucking infants was regarding him with silent hostility. In the middle of them stood a teacher with Mim, the old Mim, clinging to her skirt.

'And what do you want?' she said.

'I've come to fetch Mim – Emily,' David said, advancing. The wide-eyed babies shrank back and Mim cowered closer into the safety of the corduroy skirt.

'Emily's sister takes her home at lunchtime,' the teacher said. She was not smiling. 'Who are you?'

'I'm her brother.'

The teacher bent down and unhooked Mim from her skirt. 'Is this your brother?'

Mim grizzled and burrowed her head into the fabric. David was too surprised to lose his temper. He heard himself pleading: 'Mim, don't be daft. It's me.'

He became aware of a suspicious muttering behind him and noticed the unfriendly faces at his back. The teacher looked equally unfriendly.

'Emily came running in to the classroom and said there was a strange man hiding in the toilets. I think she'd know her own brother, don't you?'

A strange man? David was tall for his age, and among all this knee-high furniture felt taller than ever, but – a man? Then he caught sight of himself in the little mirror over the washbasins, or rather, a slice of himself; a strip of football shirt and two big red hands; and realized how the rest of him must look, hair on end, face flushed from the cold air, bare muddy knees, hockey shoes. Mim had never seen him like this before. He must look terrifying – and enormous.

'Ask Judy,' he said. 'Ask her sister – my sister. She's going on a school trip today, that's why I'm here. They're leaving at twelve,' he added, foreseeing his alibi vanish before it could be established. 'She's in 6AK, Mrs Knight's class. Please.'

A large sort of senior infant was dispatched to find Judy. 'You'd better stay here,' the teacher said, now apparently resigned to having Mim dangling from her skirt like some kind of growth. The other little ones were trickling out

of the classroom towards their mothers, giving
David an exaggeratedly wide berth. They had
been warned about strange men. David, feeling
larger, heavier and more of a fool by the minute,
stood helplessly by the door until the senior
infant returned with Judy, self-important and
cross, in his wake. She saw the teacher before
she saw David.

'Yes, Miss Craven?'

Miss Craven waved in his direction and
muttered, 'Judy, is this your brother?'

Judy turned, blinked, and said, 'Yes. Why?'

'And he's collecting Emily today?'

'Yes, I'm going on the theatre trip.' Judy
patted the lapels of her best coat, then noticed
Mim and swooped. 'Darling! What's the matter?'

'Don't set her off again, for heaven's sake,' Miss Craven said. David began to like the tone of her voice. Here was someone else who found Mim less than adorable. 'All right, Judy. Run along and catch the coach. If you'd thought to explain, this morning, none of this would have happened, would it?'

Judy, now in the wrong, shot a vengeful scowl at David and took off, the skirts of her best coat flying as she ran. Miss Craven turned her attention to Mim, who was emerging warily, like a small animal after hibernation.

'You've been rather a silly girl, haven't you?' Miss Craven remarked, coolly, and David could have hugged her. 'Now, go and get your coat on. Go *on*,' she said, sharply, as Mim seemed inclined to linger. Then she smiled at David. 'I'm sorry about that, but you know how careful we must be. I might have guessed that if Emily was involved there had to be a perfectly reasonable explanation. You are a fearsome sight, though,' she said, and, thawing entirely, laughed.

'I came straight over from games,' David said.

'You're at the big school?'

'Year 9,' David said, knowing that it would surprise her. He was feeling gigantic by now. This was almost a consolation for having to walk home through the streets in his hockey kit. Mim emerged from behind the coathooks, clutching her yellow briefcase to her chest.

'Now,' Miss Craven said, 'look hard, Emily. This is your brother, right?'

Mim looked him up and down and finally located something she could recognize, a round scar, just below his left knee.

'Yith.'

David winced at the lisp, which was not a real one, and took Mim's free hand.

'Goodbye, miss.' He edged through the milling mothers, refusing to meet their eyes, heading for the playground and the street. He did not walk slowly and Mim had to canter to keep up; but she did keep up.

They were halfway down the road before she said anything, and then she giggled.

'I thought you were a man,' she said.

David looked down at the head bobbing beside him. 'Well, I am, near enough.'

'What's that mean?'

He was so startled that he did not answer, immediately. Mim was actually talking; not performing, just talking, asking questions.

'I mean, I will be a man, soon.'

There was a short pause while she took this in.

'Can I watch?'

'Watch what?'

'When you turn into a man.'

He laughed. 'It doesn't happen all at once.'

'What happens, then?'

'I just keep growing bigger – like you.'

'Am I going to be a man?'

There she went again, spoiling it all.

'Emily!' He made himself sound stern. 'Don't be silly. You'll be a woman.'

'Will I?' She looked quite taken aback, which wasn't surprising, he reflected, given the way everyone was so set on keeping her a baby.

'Of course. You'll go on growing, too.'

'Am I growing now?'

'Yes,' he said, 'this minute. All the time. You're already bigger than you were yesterday.'

'Where?'

'All over.'

'Will you measure me when we get in?'

Three hours ago he'd have sworn that she wouldn't know what measuring meant.

'I've got to get back to school. Mum'll do it.'

'I want you to.'

'OK, Mim, but we'll have to be quick.'

'Call me Emily.'

'Right on, sister,' he said.

Left Foot Forward

Singlewell High School was small, but St George's C of E Primary had been even smaller. Waiting for his first PE lesson, feeling dwarfish in the high green vaults of the Singlewell changing room, Shaun remembered St George's and felt almost homesick.

In the doorway Mr Durkin loomed. Mr Durkin taught PE and games, and nothing else. At St George's Mrs Calloway had taken them for everything; maths and language, science, cookery, music, art – and football. There were so few of them that to get a team together they used to amalgamate with the boys from Church Whitton and even then Emily Stowe had to be goalie.

Emily was away with the girls now, mutinously playing netball. On the bus home, after the first day at Singlewell, Emily had confided to Shaun that she was going to ask Mr Durkin if she could go on with football, but Shaun, now eyeing Mr Durkin's silhouette, doubted that she would get much encouragement. Mr Durkin reminded Shaun of something out of a horror movie; not the old-fashioned kind where a mad scientist, holed up in a derelict Bavarian schloss, created an uncontrollable monster, but the type that turned up on video featuring cybernetic mutants from the future, computerized and ruthless. Seen in that light, Mr Durkin was state of the art.

By the end of the lesson, Shaun realized that he had got it all wrong. Mr Durkin was large but mild. It was Mr Prior, his sidekick, half the size but twice as noisy, who supplied the sound and the fury. Ian Edwards, from Church Whitton, remarked that Durkin and Prior were really an interrogation team, taking turns to soften you up and then rough you up. Ian did not care either way. He was sure of a place in any team going.

Mr Durkin stayed very much in the background while Mr Prior conducted the lesson with a series of barks and grunts. Mr Durkin was watchful; he was on the look-out.

Talent scout, Shaun thought; he's *noticing* people. Ian was noticed, and Tom Carter who had come to Singlewell with Shaun, from St George's. Shaun was noticed too, but in a different way. This became apparent the following Monday, when they had their first games lesson. Sides were chosen. Unlike St George's there were enough of them in the first year for two teams. Shaun was not in either. Mr Prior growled something about acquiring ball skills and sent him, with three other rejects, to kick about on a disused pitch that sloped and had outcrops of rock in it.

'We're the ones with two left feet,' said Edgar Crump, cheerfully, and acquired rock skills, while the other three deployed their six left feet with a mildewed ball that leaked air and, mysteriously, bubbles of moisture. Mr Durkin passed once in their direction, cried, 'That's right; keep it up, lads,' and swerved away again. Shaun, changing afterwards, foresaw that the rest of the term, the rest of the year, possibly the rest of his life was going to be spent like that. Edgar did not mind. He was prepared to wait until May, when his fast bowling would be revealed to the unsuspecting Prior and Durkin. The other two left-footers planned to bring along computer games next time. As far as they were concerned, Monday football constituted an extended lunch hour.

Shaun consulted his timetable and discovered that Monday afternoon was scheduled to end as badly as it had begun. The next lesson was double maths. On his last day at St George's Mrs Calloway had taken him aside and said, 'Don't worry about going to big school. You'll get on fine – but you'll have to work hard at your maths. Promise me you'll do that.'

Shaun had promised. He meant to keep his word and for the first ten minutes of the lesson he paid careful attention, sitting upright with his arms folded upon his new file, with its single sheet of paper on which he had written the date and underlined it neatly. But gradually, like drizzle, a grey memory fell before his eyes; the steep and stony pitch, the flabby ball, the clumsy rejected boots of the eight left feet; new boots, in his case. It did not matter about the others. They didn't care what they played, but he had been looking forward to the games lesson. He loved football. He hated maths. It was going to be a real effort to keep his promise to Mrs Calloway, but he loved football. It had never mattered that the combined team of St George's and Church Whitton had not won a match in three seasons; he enjoyed playing.

The next games period found the eight left feet back on the pitch of stones. Alongside them, on the real pitch, the rest of the group played a real game, while beyond that rose occasional shrieks as Emily Stowe put the fear of God into the netball players. Edgar had joined the computer freaks, so Shaun had sole possession of the ball, which was no longer round but lopsided, like the gibbous moon.

He dribbled it up and down the pitch, pirouetting round flints and tussocks and the strange scaly leaves that sprouted in clumps, alien vegetation from a distant planet. The phantom figures of twenty-one players surrounded him, but he eluded them all, scoring goal after goal. Phantom goalies flung themselves at his headers in futile dives. Phantom team-mates hugged him. Occasionally he glanced round to see if Mr Prior or Mr Durkin were looking his way. They never were.

On the way back to the changing room a row broke out. Mr Prior had been particularly noisy at close of play. 'Hark at him,' muttered a gingery boy from 7G. 'Anyone would think we were at Wembley. It's only a game.'

A fiery glow seemed to envelop Mr Prior. '*Only a game?* I can't be bothered with people who aren't prepared to give one hundred per cent and then some extra. Only a game? If that's how you feel you can go and play hopscotch. I'm sure we can find someone to take your place.'

Shaun's excitement punched him in the ribs. If they were looking for someone else to take the place of the gingery boy from 7G, there was only one other place where they could look. The same thought occurred to Mr Prior.

'So watch it,' he added lamely.

If only maths did not come next. If only the bad times did not have to happen on Monday afternoons, infecting everything that followed during the rest of the week. English was his best subject; art was fun; geography was easy. He had all three on Monday mornings, a wonderful start to the week. Kind words rang in his ears; complimentary red comments underlined his homework; a sketch of Edgar's feet, which he had knocked off in twenty minutes, ascended miraculously to a place on the wall beside some sixth-former's A-level life study. By lunchtime he ought to have been buoyant, confident, set up for success, but the praise was hollow. Beneath the buoyancy lay a dark despondent pit. His self-esteem leaked damply away. *After* lunch there was nothing to look forward to but that dismal hour on the pitch of stones, followed by a more dismal hour of maths.

Today was misty. The school, lying on a hillside above the estuary, was swept by coastal squalls, off-shore winds and sea fog. The wet air thickened, white and heavy. The farther goal vanished in the pallid murk; the adjacent pitch was invisible, although Shaun could tell how the game was going by the surge of noise, ebbing and flowing tidally in the fog; stampeding feet, the thud of boot on ball, the duetting whistles of Prior and Durkin, now close at hand, now fading eerily. Mainly the sounds were at the upper end of the pitch and his heart went out to the lonely goalie on the winning side, marooned in his net at the lower end where he waited for the ball to emerge from the vapour.

After that, the first five minutes of the maths lesson were almost enjoyable. All the lights were on, the radiators were hot. Shaun snuggled down in his corner seat and thawed contentedly, but it could not last. Homework was being handed back. Little was said, but people were looking congratulations at each other as Miss Stevens prowled the classroom, doling out sheets of paper.

Just proving she knows our names already,' said Ian in front, over his shoulder. 'Show-off.'

'I knew *yours* on the first day,' Miss Stevens said, slapping down his paper in front of him. 'We always notice the loudmouths first. Well done, anyway.'

Ian grinned and turned to pick up his paper.

Shaun saw the short hairs on the back of his neck bristle with pride – but now it was Shaun's turn, the last paper of all, limp and forlorn. Shaun looked up at its underside and recognized one of his own dirty thumb prints between Miss Stevens's clean fingertips.

'You don't really seem to have got the hang of this,' Miss Stevens said, laying the paper on his desk so that he could see all the red writing, none of it complimentary this time, that covered it. 'I'll have a word with you at the end of the lesson.'

'Have you always found maths difficult?' Miss Stevens asked, at the end of the lesson.

Shaun nodded, although it was not strictly true. Years ago it had seemed as easy as anything else, in the infants, when it was just something that he did, in those days before it sneakily detached itself from the rest of his education and became maths. But Miss Stevens had BSc. after her name and would not know about the infants.

'Yes, miss,' he said.

Miss Stevens looked kind; sad, but kind. 'I suppose you're one of the bus people.'

He could not see what that had to do with it, whizz-kid Ian was a bus person and it did not seem to do his maths any harm. What he could see, out in the fog, were the headlights of the bus itself, and he had about three minutes in which to catch it.

'Yes, miss.'

'Well then, I can't suggest that you stop after school for extra tuition – some people do that. But you do need help. Are you in the band – or gym club?'

'No, miss.' She certainly did know how to stray off the subject.

'Then you'd better come along to my room tomorrow lunchtime. We'll see how that goes for a few weeks, shall we?'

She was doing him a favour, he knew that. He made a grateful noise and backed out of the room, racing for the cloakroom and then the bus, where Emily Stowe was cock-a-hoop, running up and down the gangway and punching the air. She had been sent off, during netball. No one in the history of the school, she thought, had ever had a red card in netball.

'It wasn't a foul, though,' she explained, settling next to Shaun as the bus started. 'I'd never do nothing like that. I just throw the ball too hard and no one can catch it. They fall over.'

She tried to sound remorseful, but Shaun could envision the other netball players, felled like skittles by Emily's demon delivery.

'I've got to do extra maths,' Shaun said.

'What, for homework?' Emily said. 'I'll help. I'll do it for you.' She had done a lot of it for him at St George's, too. That had been part of the trouble.

'No, at school, Tuesday lunchtime,' Shaun

said and saw, with sinking spirits, how the awfulness of Monday was spilling over into Tuesday; how soon, like a creeping paralysis, it would take over Wednesday, and Thursday too, until it ruined the whole week.

When, on the following Monday, Shaun looked at the classroom calendar before registration, he realized that there were only two weeks left before half-term. He had heard somewhere that time passes more quickly as you get older. His life was skidding away from under him, and he knew why. At St George's he had taken one day at a time because, except for birthdays and Christmas, or bad moments due to his own villainy, one day had been as good as another. But now he spent his time wishing that Monday was over, even as early as the previous Tuesday. Life had been reduced to a series of Mondays; he scarcely noticed what came in between.

It was a frosty day, clear and bright. From the pitch of stones he could see the estuary glinting in the distance. Weak but well-intentioned sunlight gilded the smoke stacks on the cement works. It was too cold to stand about so the other left feet abandoned the computer games and joined Shaun with the bad-news ball; not the original one which had collapsed altogether and gone strangely stiff, but a replacement, equally limp and soggy. Shaun suspected that somewhere there was a factory turning out special partially-collapsed footballs for people like him.

Indoors again, after they had changed, Mr Durkin read out a list of names. Mr Prior stood by, casting a watchful eye over them.

'All these boys,' he said, 'will report here for extra coaching on Wednesday lunchtimes.' Shaun mentally reviewed the list. Ian Edwards and Tom Carter were on it, even the gingery boy from 7G. Edgar Crump was not, nor was Shaun, nor any of the other left feet. Those who were on it smiled at each other.

'What's them two so pleased with themselves about?' asked Emily Stowe, later, on the bus, as Tom and Ian toasted each other in Seven-Up.

'They've been picked for extra football,' Shaun said.

'I'm going to be let do hockey after half-term,' Emily said, 'with the Year 8s.' She paused and thought. 'Why're they doing extra football?'

'Because they're good at it,' Shaun said. 'For the team.'

'But that's not why you get extra maths, is it?' Emily said. 'You get extra maths because you're not good at it.'

Shaun felt his gloom pierced by a needle of resentment.

'Yes,' he said.

'Well that's not fair is it?' Emily said. 'You get extra maths because you can't do it, and they get extra football because they can.'

Shaun's needle became a bodkin, then a six-inch nail.

'If I was you,' Emily advised, with an evil smile, 'I'd ask old Durkin if you can have extra football too.'

He knew that she was not really concerned on his behalf. He had once heard Mrs Calloway describe Emily Stowe as a stirrer. She was stirring now. She liked the idea of a fight.

'You ask him, on Wednesday,' she said. 'I'll come with you.'

Shaun thought that this last was the least attractive proposition he had heard in a long while. But the one before it had certain possibilities.

'I'll ask him by myself,' he said.

'I'll watch,' said Emily.

* * *

Tuesday's extra maths tuition was not a success. Shaun's mind was on other things. On Wednesday, with Emily at a constant but safe distance, he went along to the changing room, carrying his kit.

Mr Durkin never changed, nor Mr Prior. They seemed to live in their tracksuits, appearing in them for games and PE, at registration and assembly, Mr Prior's small and purple, Mr Durkin's large and black. Shaun approached the large black tracksuit.

'Sir?'

'Now, what do you want?' Mr Durkin asked. 'This is extra coaching time.'

'Yes,' Shaun said. 'I know. I want to do extra coaching.'

'No, no,' said Mr Durkin, good-humouredly, as if explaining to an idiot something very obvious, such as how button-holes work. 'This is for the boys who will be in the team.'

'Yes. I want to be in the team,' Shaun said.

He could see Mr Durkin's problem. If Shaun went on like this Mr Durkin would be forced to say, out loud, that Shaun had two left feet and might just as well be applying to join the England squad. Out of the corner of his eye he could also see, through the frosted glass panel of the door, Emily Stowe, eavesdropping, longing to rush in and speak up for him. He had to speak up for himself before Emily burst through the door (not bothering to open it but leaving an Emily-shaped hole in the glass, like Desperate Dan) and gazed unblushingly at Ian Edwards and Tom Carter with no trousers on.

'Look, sir,' said Shaun, 'I have to do extra maths with Miss Stevens so I can get good at it. I want to get good at football. I want to do extra, like the others.'

Mr Prior, at this point, might have exploded and seriously damaged Shaun in the blast, but Mr Durkin, fatally, gave himself time to think.

'I'm never going to get good if I don't practise, am I, sir?' Shaun said.

'No one is stopping you from practising,' Mr Durkin said.

'I can't practise on my own,' Shaun persisted, 'not on that horrible old pitch with that horrible old ball. Not with people who don't care anyway. I want to play properly. I don't see why I shouldn't do it at all just because I don't do it well. I mean—' he pressed home his advantage '—I mean, I couldn't go to Miss Stevens and say I wasn't going to do that extra maths 'cause I'm no good anyway, could I, sir?'

'That's a bit different,' Mr Durkin said. 'Maths is important. After all, football's only—'

He stopped. He did not say it. Just in time he saw the trap, and it was his own mouth. Then he looked round and saw Mr Prior. Shaun fancied that he detected a light sweat breaking out on Mr Durkin's forehead.

'What's this lad up to?' Mr Prior asked. 'Giving trouble?'

'Not at all,' said Mr Durkin. 'He's just come along to watch the coaching. I think,' said Mr Durkin, and Shaun could see him thinking, 'that shows real enthusiasm, don't you?'

'Yes!' cried Mr Prior, with no enthusiasm at all. He wheeled, and bolted back to the players. 'Come on, boys. Outside in five seconds flat!'

'Enthusiasm ... important attitude ... essential to team spirit,' Mr Durkin was chuntering. 'Remind me at the start of the lesson next Monday. I'll see that you get a game – time we tried out some of you others ... oh.' He hesitated. 'I suppose there's no chance that the rest think as you do?' Shaun smiled kindly.

'What, Edgar and that? Oh no, sir, just me ... I think,' he added, and had the satisfaction of seeing Mr Durkin cringe at the prospect of Edgar and the other left feet taking steps to improve their game.

Uncle Matthew

Lucy, sit down for a moment, I need to talk to you. If your friend's waiting he can wait a bit longer. In any case, I don't see any friends out there, unless—

Look, Lucy, when I was your age – don't kick the skirting board like that. Sit down. This isn't going to be a lecture, it's a story, and I meant what I said. I was exactly your age.

It was two days after my birthday and I went into town to buy some new football boots. Dad – your grandpa – had given me the money for them as a birthday present. He'd promised me the boots but Mum – Granny – said, 'You'd better wait till September before you buy them, the rate your feet are growing.' She was just thinking of games lessons at school, but my dad knew that I needed them that minute. We played football all year round, of course we did. Outside of school there was no cricket season for us.

It was June so there were no sales on – no, there *weren't*, not in those days. Sales happened in January and July. Anyway, the sports shop had none I could afford so I went over to Debenhams, where they had a big shoe department.

Lucy, I know you're not interested in football, but just listen.

It was like our Debenhams, not quite so big, but like a maze inside. You had to work your way through the perfume department and ladies' hosiery, handbags – you know how it is, and it was all bright lights with mirrors everywhere; little ones on the make-up counters, tall tilted ones among the shoe racks, big oblong ones on the pillars that held up the ceiling. Everywhere I looked I could see myself coming or going, sometimes three or four of me, from the side, from the back, all heading in different directions. And I noticed something that I didn't usually see – when one mirror reflected another, I saw myself as I really was, not back to front, like when you look directly at yourself in the glass.

The first time, I couldn't think what was strange about it, then I started to experiment. I shut my left eye and the face in the mirror shut its left eye. Usually when you do that, the mirror image shuts its right eye.

I forgot all about the boots. I just wandered around, tracking myself from mirror to mirror, making faces, waving my hands. I'm surprised the store detective didn't follow me in case I went completely mad and started smashing things. Maybe he did – I never saw him.

But what I did see, in a little mirror on the

glove counter, was me looking over my own shoulder, and then the second face slid out of sight, which wouldn't have bothered me except that I hadn't moved.

I turned round. A little way off, between two racks of coats, was a glass that showed me full-length. I'd wandered into the menswear section by that time. It was darker there and they didn't have so many mirrors. Well, I stood and looked at myself and then I raised my right arm and saluted. The boy in the mirror raised *his* right arm and saluted back. That shook me because I was standing dead in front of this mirror, only two or three metres away from it, so it had to be reflecting *me*, not reflecting a reflection of me. So I took a step forward, and the reflection took a step back. I went cold then; something was wrong, something was terribly wrong. I couldn't move. But the reflection moved, it shrugged its shoulders, turned and walked away, sort of nodding at me to follow. It was limping. I wasn't limping, and I saw that where the reflection had been, there was no mirror at all, just a big white sign with black letters saying VISIT OUR NEW COFFEE SHOP ON THE SECOND FLOOR.

I didn't want to visit anything; all I wanted to do was get out, but I was too shaken to move. I wasn't frightened yet, but I was shivering, standing there alone between the two rows of coats, all those shoulders level with my eyes, like standing between two ranks of soldiers and nothing in front of me but that notice: VISIT OUR NEW COFFEE SHOP ON THE SECOND FLOOR.

Then all the shoulders on the right started heaving. Someone on the other side of the row was riffling through the hangers, and somebody pushed behind me and I unfroze. I turned round then and went back out, not running, sort of floating through all the mirrors, watching myself coming and going in my blue jeans and white T-shirt. And as I went, I realized what had seemed so wrong before. The person who had confronted me between those coat racks, he had had my face, but he hadn't worn my clothes.

He'd been wearing short trousers, fairly short, just above the knee – yes, I know shorts come down to the knee these days, but they didn't in 1969. Shorts were short, and no one wore them in the street, no one my age. And he'd worn a grey shirt and a grey knitted pullover and long grey socks. And a tie, a sort of school tie, with stripes. If he hadn't looked like me, he'd have looked like William – you know, William Brown and the Outlaws, in the books. But he didn't have a cap on.

I went home. Mum said, 'Didn't you get the boots, then?' and I said, no, I'd decided to do what she'd said and wait till September.

My voice sounded strange. She looked at me hard and said, 'You've been out in the sun too long. You're as white as a sheet.'

I tried to be funny. 'I ought to be brown if I've been out in the sun too long, oughtn't I?' But I've never been brown. People with hair the colour of mine don't tan; we stay pale or we burn. That boy I'd seen in Debenhams, he'd had my hair; my hair and my face.

I've never believed stories about people who meet their doubles, because most of the time you'd never recognize your double. What you see in the mirror isn't what other people see. By now, I didn't know *what* I'd seen, *who* I'd seen, and when Mum sent me to lie down I went into the bedroom and hung a sweater over the mirror so that I wouldn't have to see it again.

I couldn't go on avoiding mirrors for ever, the house was full of them: one on the wall of the bathroom, Dad's shaving mirror with the magnifying glass that made you look like the creature from 20,000 fathoms, two in the hall, one over the mantelpiece in the front room, a little one in the kitchen and two or three in my parents' room. Very gradually I brought myself to start looking in them, but the only face that looked back was mine. It raised its right eyebrow when I raised my left. I suppose I was hoping to discover that it was all a trick of the light, but I wasn't really fooling myself. What I'd seen in the menswear section hadn't been in a mirror at all.

Mum kept me in for a couple of days and then the weather broke. We had a thunderstorm and it got cooler. One evening I went down to the rec on my bike with my old boots slung around my neck. I just fancied a good kick-about in the mud. All my mates were there and we belted up and down for about an hour. It started to rain again, but we didn't care. It felt like the real thing, after the heatwave; mud and rain and a soggy wet football.

As I said, all my mates were there, and one other. I didn't notice him at first, we were all pounding up and down, skidding about, falling over. Although it was almost mid-summer, the clouds were so heavy that the air was dark and thick, more like an autumn evening. The rain came down harder, and in the end we packed up and wandered off in twos and threes. I sat down on a bench to change back into my shoes, and when I looked up I saw someone standing on the path that led between the rec and the allotments. It ran from Church Lane to the main road, and on one side there was a chain-link fence that was all trodden down where we took short cuts into the rec.

In his grey shirt and sweater and shorts, and his long grey socks, he was the same colour as the twilight. He wasn't transparent, but I couldn't see which side of the fence he was standing. And that's all he did. When I raised my right hand to wave, he just stood. We weren't playing games now.

I called out to him, 'What do you want?' because that's what I felt, that he wanted something.

He didn't answer, but he looked me full in the face, as he'd done before. And now we were away from all those mirrors he looked more like me than ever, but not exactly like me. He was thinner and taller, but otherwise pale and freckled ... with that red hair. Only his was cut short and clippered up the back. I wore mine long like footballers did – like everyone did then.

I yelled at him, 'Why don't you leave me alone?' but he just smiled, as he'd done before, in Debenhams, and turned his back.

I'd told him to leave me alone, but I didn't like it when he started walking away. I jumped over the fence where it was squashed flat, and went after him; left the boots and the bike and chased him down the footpath. He didn't seem to be running – he was still limping – but I couldn't catch up. He was always ahead of me and I saw nothing else, just that grey figure in the rain. I saw nothing else when we got down to the main road, I didn't even see the road, till someone shouted and grabbed me by the shoulder, just as I was running across the pavement, just as I was about to run straight under a lorry. I saw these great wheels go by, as tall as I was, and a frightened, yelling woman who'd dropped all her parcels in a puddle to drag me to safety.

'What were you doing? What did you think you were doing?' she kept saying, and shaking me. She was crying with fright. In the end I sort of came round and said something about some big boys chasing me.

But I was the one who'd been doing the chasing, and the person I'd chased was standing on the other side of the road, watching us. I knew she hadn't seen *him*.

I don't remember going back to the rec, but I must have done, because when I got home I was wheeling my bike with the boots dangling from the crossbar.

Mum was out, round at a friend's, when I got in, but Dad was there. They'd never have left me to come home to an empty house, thank God.

He sent me off to get changed – it was raining stair rods by then and I was soaked. When I came down again he'd made me some drinking chocolate and he said, 'As I understand it, that's the second time in a week you've come home looking like death warmed up. What's the matter?'

How could I tell him? I didn't know *what* to tell him, but I knew he was keeping an eye on me, after that.

I was keeping an eye on me, too, in the mirror, in all the mirrors. But the next time I saw my grey friend it was out of doors again, on the cradle bridge over the railway. That was what we called it, a footbridge made of iron girders, high up over a cutting where the line came out of some woodland.

I usually cycled to school, but I'd got a puncture, so I took the short cut over the bridge that day. I was walking on my own, and as I came towards the bridge it seemed to be empty, but as soon as I set foot on it I saw him, at the far end, just climbing up onto the girders. He gripped the handrail, swung his leg over behind, as if he was getting on a bike, and then seemed to be on the other side of the girders, and vanished.

I kept walking towards the end of the bridge. The sun was shining where I was, I remember my shadow beside me on the wooden boards, but his end was shaded by trees. When I reached the place where he had been sitting I looked over, and there he was on the side of the cutting, down below. He saw me watching and waved, beckoning.

But this time he had given me too much warning, he had moved too soon, for when the express from Dover came thundering round the curve, he was dancing on the rails in front of it. But I was still at the top of the cutting. I don't recall doing it, but I had climbed up the girders and over the side of the bridge.

I didn't go to school. If I'd thought that I should find my mother at home, I'd have hidden in the woods all day, but she was at work. It was my father I wanted to talk to, and I knew where to find him. He worked shifts, and when he was on nights he went straight from the factory to put in an hour or two on our allotment, the one next to the rec.

I had something to ask him that I couldn't bring myself to ask Mum.

As I stumbled along the grass paths I could see him by the little shed he had built from old railway sleepers, drinking tea from his thermos and smoking a cigarette.

He might have said, 'Why aren't you at school?' but he had more sense than that. He just looked at me and said, 'Hm, three frights in a row. Now will you let on?' He poured some more tea and gave me the cup.

I said, 'Dad, tell me, please, was I ever a twin?' For that was what I'd been wondering, what I'd been sure of, that I must have been born with a brother, a brother who had died before I could know him and had now come back to haunt me, a brother my age who looked just like me.

Dad lit another cigarette, then he said, 'No, you were never a twin. But I was.'

Now, Lucy, you've got all your grandparents, two of each, but I had only my mother's mum for a gran and Dad didn't have anyone by the time I came along.

'I was the younger one, Mark,' my dad said. 'Matthew was seventeen minutes older. We were inseparable, went everywhere together, did everything together; except once. We came through the war without a scratch, even though we lived in South London, but a year before it ended, 1944, I went to a party without him. He'd sprained his foot and couldn't walk much. I wanted to stay home with him, but he said, "No, you go. One of the sisters is engaged to a Yank. You might get some chewing gum."

'When I came home, the house had gone. Half the street had gone. A flying bomb had cut out overhead. We all lost someone. I lost my parents, my grandparents, and my brother Matthew, my twin.'

He was put in a home, he said. And then he told me that for the rest of that year he kept seeing Matthew, at the home, at school, in the street, limping ahead of him, and always Matthew was smiling, waving, beckoning him to follow. And at first he did follow, but then he began to notice that the places Matthew beckoned him towards were not very safe places; scrap yards, railway lines, busy roads. In the end, after he'd nearly broken his neck falling down a cellar on a bomb site where Matthew had led him, he decided that next time Matthew called him he would stay put. And he said that Matthew kept trying, but after this he started getting harder to see and in the end, after about a year, after their next birthday, Matthew disappeared altogether.

'And now he seems to be back,' Dad said to me. 'Well, he'd every reason to want me to join him, but he's got no call to fetch *you* away. What's he tried so far?'

So I told him about the lorry, and the cradle bridge. 'But he's not like you, Dad,' I said. 'Even his hair's different.'

'Oh, no,' my dad said, 'we weren't identical twins. You're not much like me, either, but you're just like him.'

And as he said it, I looked up, and saw Matthew, my uncle, a little way off in an old greenhouse. There was mainly just the frame left but I knew it was full of broken glass, like razors.

And for about a year afterwards, just as my dad had done, I saw Matthew here and there, always smiling, always beckoning, always limping, wearing his shorts and his shirt, his pullover and his long grey socks. I never followed him again.

You've seen him too, haven't you? Oh, Lucy, don't deny it. You've never been one for dangerous games; no climbing trees or walking on walls for you; not even rough sports. You're happiest with your Sindy dolls and little ponies.

But Lucy, I saw you on your birthday, fooling on the rails by the mill dam. I saw you yesterday on your bike, on the slip road to the motorway.

Where were you going today with your friend, your friend who is waiting, the friend I cannot see? I haven't seen him for twenty-six years, since he was eleven, since I was eleven, since I was your age. I told you, didn't I; exactly your age.

Oh, darling, don't follow him, do as I did, do as my father did. Smile and walk away. He wants you to join him, as he wanted us, but don't do it, don't do it.

We'll all join him eventually. He will just have to wait.

About the Author

Jan Mark is one of today's most distinguished writers for young people. Her work includes picture books, story collections, novels, non-fiction and television and radio scripts. She has won many awards (including the Carnegie Medal twice) and has been shortlisted for countless others. Some of her best-known books include *Thunder and Lightnings*, *Handles* and *Nothing to be Afraid Of*. More recently, she has written the highly-acclaimed novels *The Eclipse of the Century*, *The Lady with Iron Bones*, *Long Lost* and *Something in the Air*. Jan Mark was born in Welwyn Garden City and now lives in Oxford. She writes full-time and regularly visits schools to talk about her writing.

About Eyes Wide Open, Jan Mark says ...

'A novel gives a writer plenty of room to operate in. Short stories work the other way round. You haven't got room for anything that doesn't matter. So instead of creating strange new worlds you take a few days, or hours, out of a person's life and show something happening to them. It may not be Earth-shattering or dramatic, but afterwards, nothing will ever be quite the same again.'